On a rancho, sun bleached and dry, in the Mexican state of Hidalgo, lived a poor farmer and his gentle wife. Their only child was a daughter. "She is sweeter than a cactus bloom in early spring," the townsfolk said. Her name was Domitila.

The family worked hard to build their small adobe casa. Domitila learned from her parents how to make bricks by selecting soil with just the right amount of clay and sand. First, they added water from the cistern. Then, they folded in straw from the old, empty sheep stall to add strength. While they laid the squares in tidy rows to bake in the sun, Mama told Domitila their family stories from long ago. Then as Mama always did, she reminded Domitila, "Remember, my daughter, what my mother told me and her mother told her. Do every task with care, and always add a generous dash of love."

They stacked the bricks one row on top of another to build the casa walls. Carefully, they left a window opening so they could see the majestic Sierra Madre mountains in the distance.

"If only I had some new wool, I would weave you a beautiful shawl, Mama," Domitila said. "The border would be like our purple Sierras with a sunset sky of rose and gold yarn."

One day, while Domitila and her parents were working at their leather-making, creating beautiful sandals and money pouches, the sky suddenly darkened. Rain fell violently in the mountains. Water rushed down the canyons and spread across the plains, sweeping away their tiny patch of corn. Their adobe casa began to crumble.

Soon all that remained standing of the little house were two walls where the roof had not caved in. The floor was damp. The air was musty. Domitila's mother shivered and coughed.

"Mama," Domitila asked softly, "how can I help you?"

Mama was too sick to reply.

"It's hopeless," Domitila's father sighed as he looked about their home. "The bricks won't hold their shape until they have dried, and the rain clouds keep gathering. Domitila, you could help if you would go to the Governor's mansion. I hear they are paying well for kitchen workers to prepare for banquets. With what you earn, we can buy food to last until we plant some corn again. Don't worry about Mama or the house. I will take care of them."

Determined to help her poor family, Domitila wrapped her worn shawl around herself and kissed her parents goodbye. Through the blowing rain, Domitila set off for the grand mansion of the Governor of Hidalgo.

When Domitila arrived at the great house, the chief cook put her right to work. Day after day Domitila worked in the kitchen of the noble family, and day after day she dreamed of returning home to help her own poor family.

The time came when the chief cook called to Domitila, "Girl, you have shown yourself to be a fine cook. Now make something to please old Abuela and her grandson. They are eating alone this evening."

Domitila set right to work. She prepared one of her family's favorite dishes, and the maid carried the platter to the great dining room.

"What is this?" asked Timoteo, the handsome eldest son of the Governor. "I have never seen anything like this before," he scowled. "Call in the cook!"

Domitila came from the kitchen. She stood in the shadow of the great dining room doors, frightened and shy. "Speak up," snapped the young man. "What is on this platter?"

"They are nopales, Señor," she said, her head lowered in respect. "They are a prized food of my people."

"Nopales? You call nopales a prized food? They are nothing but prickly, dusty desert weeds!"

Timoteo's rude words roused his old grandmother, who had dozed off at the table while waiting to be served.

"Grandson, be polite," she scolded. "We are a noble family. We must never complain about the food of common people. Show the young girl respect and try some of what she has made."

Timoteo replied quickly, "I am sorry, Abuela." Then he made himself look contrite, and with his fork he served himself the very tiniest piece of the nopales on the platter. Trying to hide his disgust, he looked away, puckered his face, and forced the cactus into his mouth. But no sooner did the flavor

touch his tongue than his surly ways softened.

"Why, this is delicious!" He took another bite and exclaimed, "This weed has been turned into a delicacy! What is your secret?"

"I do not have a secret, Señor. I cook the way my mother taught me." Then, with her head still lowered, she slipped from the shadow of the great doorway and returned to her chores.

Timoteo took no notice of her leaving. He devoured all the mouth-watering nopales on the platter. Rubbing his stomach, he marveled to himself, "I have never felt so good. I must find out what is in this food."

A TASK WELL DONE CANNOT BE HIDDEN.

That night as Domitila lay sleeping, a servant awakened her with a message. "Your mother is seriously ill. You must return home immediately."

Domitila gathered a few things into her shawl, explained her plight to another cook, and hurriedly set out before dawn for the long journey home.

Domitila's heart nearly stopped when she came to her little house and saw her father leaning sadly against the door. "Father, how is Mama?" Domitila asked fearfully.

"Domitila," her father stammered sorrowfully, "Mama . . . Mama has passed away."

"Oh, Father, if only I could have come home earlier," Domitila sobbed as she ran to where she had last seen her mother. She sank down on the floor by the empty bed, her head in her hands.

Through her grief, Domitila felt a warm presence. Looking up, she blinked her eyes, then blinked again. There before her appeared her mother's spirit.

Domitila sat transfixed as the spirit spoke, "I will always be with you, my child, and remember what my mother told me, and her mother told her. Do every task with care, and always add a generous dash of love."

For a time, the tenderness of her mother's smile lingered. Then her spirit faded away. Domitila knew she would never forget her mother's words.

The next morning at the Governor's mansion, Timoteo returned to the dining hall. He expected a breakfast as marvelous as his dinner of nopales the evening before. Eagerly, he took a huge bite from the plate set before him. Suddenly, he clutched his throat.

"Is this a trick?" Timoteo gasped. He shouted at the maid, "Send in that cook!"

Third Cook appeared in the doorway.

With great gulps of tea, Timoteo soothed his mouth enough to speak. "Did I talk to you yesterday?" He scowled at her, unsure of which of his family's many cooks had stood in the shadow of the doors the evening before.

"No, Señor, it was Second Cook with whom you spoke yesterday. She was called home in the night because her mother is very sick." Then trying to take Timoteo's mind off her own wretched cooking, Third Cook timidly spoke up, "Second Cook left in such a hurry, she did not notice that she dropped this." From her pocket, Third Cook took a leather strip which appeared to have fallen from Domitila's sandal.

Timoteo looked closely at the leather piece. Its surface was finely carved, and the design was a chorus of flowing strokes. "Can this also be the work of that girl?" he murmured.

"She said her mother and her mother's mother taught her many skills," Third Cook added hesitantly. "She talked about adding something very special to whatever she did, but I do not know what she meant, Señor."

Timoteo was puzzled. His thoughts felt like clouds tumbling across the Sierra Madres. "Tell me," he asked Third Cook, "where does the girl live?" Timoteo had to know.

"I do not know, Señor. All she mentioned was a ranch someplace in Hidalgo far away from here."

"Except for the mountains, nearly all of Hidalgo is ranch land," shrugged the arrogant young man.

"This is all I know, Señor," said Third Cook as she backed toward the door, bowed deeply, and hurried to the kitchen.

Timoteo ran his fingers over the exquisitely carved leather piece. He rubbed his empty stomach. *If I can find the girl, surely I can learn her secret,* he thought.

"Saddle my horse," he called to one of his stablemen.

Hearing of Timoteo's rash decision, old Abuela removed a delicately embroidered silk shawl from her shoulders. "This mantón has been in our family for generations," she said as she handed it over to Timoteo. "If you must go, take it, and know that my love goes with you."

Timoteo tucked Abuela's shawl under his serape and set out for the great plains of Hidalgo. Along the way the headstrong young man asked if anyone had seen the young girl who could turn desert weeds into food fit for kings and scraps of leather into works of art. All had heard of the girl and could tell him more stories of her many talents, but no one knew where she could be found.

Timoteo rode his horse across the desert to the west, but Domitila had walked east to her home. In time Timoteo's search became the gossip of all the pueblos in the vast state of Hidalgo.

On his journey Timoteo came upon the widow Malvina outside of her hut. "Buenos dias, Señora!" Timoteo called out. "Do you know the girl of many talents? The one who can make delicacies from desert weeds?"

Hmm, thought Malvina to herself, *so this is the rich young man who is looking for Domitila. Who, in these parts, does not know about Domitila? I hear her mother died, may her soul rest in peace. Now, if I plan this right, I will win this young man for my own daughter, instead.*

EL PIE SIGUE EL CAMINO DEL CORAZÓN.

"As a matter of fact," Malvina said to Timoteo, "I do know where the girl lives." And the woman proceeded to give Timoteo careful instructions, all in the wrong direction. *Ha*, thought Malvina, *that should keep him riding in circles long enough for me to set up my plan. Then he will see who the real cook is.*

WHERE THE HEART LEANS, THE FOOT FOLLOWS.

"Thank you, Señora," said Timoteo. But, as soon as he left following the widow's directions, Malvina ran to her daughter Pereza, who was lying in the shade of a dry arbusto bush.

"Wake up, you lazy girl! We are going to be rich." Malvina shouted. Pulling Pereza by the ear, the cunning widow set off for a nearby pueblo. "Do exactly what I tell you to do," she ordered.

In no time at all, the evil Malvina had pushed the lazy Pereza from casa to casa in the little town. While Pereza begged and whined for food at the front door of each house, Malvina crept to the back and stole from the kitchens of the kindly townsfolk.

Back at their hut, Malvina built a fire and ordered Pereza to cook. They cooked all through the night and into the next day. "Finally," Malvina said smugly, "we are ready!" Off they went with jugs balanced on their heads and baskets on each arm. On a tattered serape they dragged piles of tortillas, enchiladas, tamales, and chili rellenos, all made from the stolen food. They walked across field after field to the rancho of Domitila's father.

When Malvina and Pereza arrived at the widower's casa, they found no one home. They snooped in every cupboard to see if there was food in the house. With a pleased smirk Malvina announced, "There is not a scrap of food in this place." She set about laying out all they had brought.

When Domitila and her father returned from visiting Mama's grave, they were shocked. Piled high on the table, and even on the chairs, was food of every kind. The cunning Malvina and her daughter stood nearby, pretending to show sympathy. Domitila and her father, their hearts full of grief, politely ate the tasteless, miserable meal made from stolen food.

In very little time, Malvina's scheme began to work even better than she had planned. Domitila's father missed having someone to care for him so much that he married the woman. Sadly, Domitila would now have to serve her new stepmother and stepsister.

Aha, thought Malvina, *now that I have won the widower and all his land, it will be a simple trick to fool that rich young man when he finally makes his way to this casa. I will send Domitila out to tend the pigs and be rid of her. Then I will serve him Domitila's cooking and let him think it is all Pereza's talent.*

When autumn came, life turned even harder for Domitila. "Make more bricks," her stepmother ordered. "I want a bigger house! Find more wool, Pereza needs a new shawl!" From that day on, Domitila learned what it was like to work without laughter and without her mother's encouraging words.

While Domitila waited on her cruel stepmother and on lazy Pereza, Timoteo followed Malvina's tangled directions. The young man traveled through the early fall rains and shivered in his wet serape. He became more and more spellbound by each wondrous story he was told about the talented girl as he rode along the way. The once proud Timoteo pushed on, cold and hungry. He thought to himself, *perhaps there is far more to know about this poor girl than merely the good taste of her cooking.* But none of the travelers he met could tell him exactly where the girl lived in the endless desert ranch lands of Hidalgo. Timoteo ran his fingers across the designs carved on the leather piece. *I will never stop until I find her,* Timoteo resolved as he urged his horse on.

One day Timoteo heard music in the distance. In his long travels he had come upon the grand Hidalgo Fall Fiesta. As he approached, he could not believe the familiar fragrance in the air. Was he coming closer to what he had been seeking? Timoteo spurred his horse to a gallop. This turn of events was not a part of Malvina's plan.

The young man called out to the women at the Fiesta, "Where is the person who cooks nopales so delicious I could smell them miles away?" The women saw that the handsome Timoteo held the piece of leather with the designs they all recognized as Domitila's beautiful work.

"You must mean the girl called Domitila," the women all talked at once. They told him Domitila made her nopales for every Fall Fiesta and that the desert winds carried their fragrance for miles around. "That is why we are sold out just now," they said. "They are so delicious, folks come for them from far away."

An elderly woman spoke above the others, "Of course, people in these parts know what makes the girl's nopales so flavorful. They know about the care she gives to all her work and the very special love she puts into everything she does."

At this, a kindly old woman tending a food booth added, "If it is Domitila you are looking for, son, she is not here. She left to visit her mother's grave. The trail is easy if you wish to find her. Just follow the creek."

The young man thanked everyone graciously for helping him, and set out once again. He pondered what was said about Domitila as he followed the simple words of the kindly old woman. Aware, now, that Malvina had always pointed him the wrong way, Timoteo rode confidently in the opposite direction.

Far ahead just as the old woman had said, Timoteo saw a young girl walking.

"Buenos dias, Señorita!" he called out to the girl, urging his horse to go faster.

When Timoteo reached her, he dismounted and asked, "I have been searching for a girl called Domitila. Do you know where I can find her?"

Still holding the carved strip of leather, Timoteo looked down and saw the girl wearing sandals with a matching design. As she looked up at him, a gentle breeze lifted her hair from her beautiful face. For the first time, they looked into each other's eyes. Just as the sun bursts above the Sierra peaks to start a new day, Timoteo's search had come to an end. "You are Domitila!" he exclaimed.

"Señor, you have traveled so far, you must be very hungry," said Domitila, as she saw how thin the handsome son of the Governor had grown from his long ride through the harsh desert weather. She untied her scarf and took out a tortilla filled with her delicious nopales.

Domitila and Timoteo sat down in the shade by the stream. Timoteo told her how he had searched for her throughout Hidalgo and how he had met the widow Malvina, who led him astray. Then Domitila understood Malvina's dark plot and how it had reached all the way to snare the son of the Governor, her own father, and even herself.

Together they broke open the tortilla. Its fragrance drifted up and encircled them. As he tasted her food once again, Timoteo suddenly understood the secret of the nopales. *So this is what people mean by their amazing stories about Domitila,* thought Timoteo as his heart softened. *Certainly this must be what the women at the Fiesta were trying to tell me, and what the cook was attempting to say back at the hacienda. Desert weeds can become a banquet when they are made by Domitila. But, it is her love that makes them fill my heart.*

Timoteo marveled at the girl. Then he took out Abuela's exquisitely embroidered shawl. Tenderly, he placed the shimmering silk around Domitila's shoulders.

Domitila and Timoteo went on to visit Mama's grave, as they would every year from that time on. And as the welcome shadows of the Sierra Madre cooled the desert heat, they set off toward the capital of Hidalgo. They went directly to the Governor's mansion, but this time Domitila did not return as a servant; she returned to become Timoteo's lovely bride.

In due season, Timoteo became the Governor of Hidalgo. The kind ways his wife had taught him brought prosperity and good will to all the citizens of the land. The wicked Malvina and the lazy Pereza fled from Hidalgo. Father moved into the mansion to be reunited with his daughter and her new family.

As for Domitila, old Abuela's silk shawl shimmered around her shoulders as the family gathered to eat her delicious nopales by the warmth of the fire in the great room of the Governor's mansion. Abuela dozed contentedly nearby.

While Timoteo bounced their little ones on his knees, he smiled as Domitila told them over and over what her mother used to tell her, "Do every task with care, my children, and never, ever forget to add a generous dash of love."

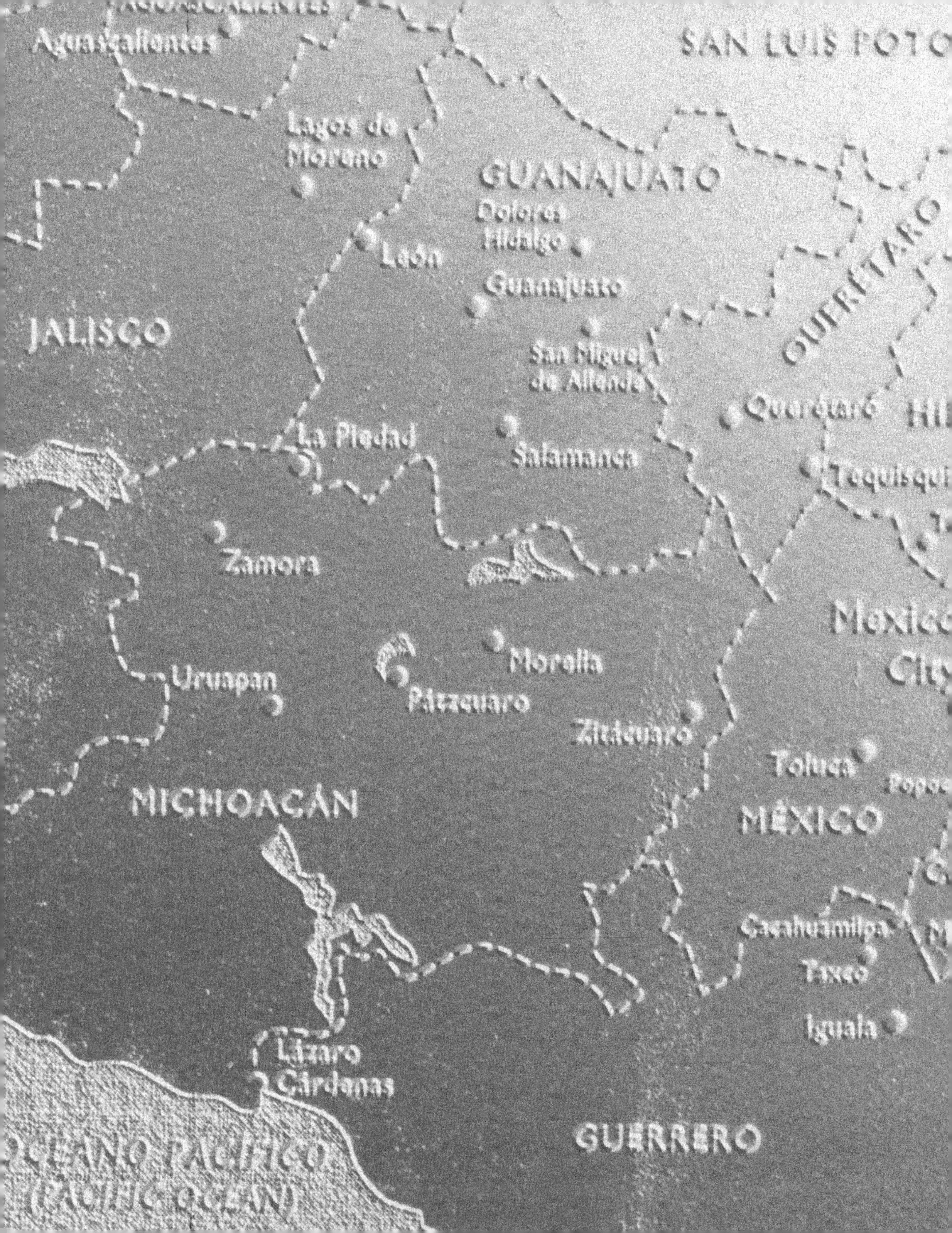
Aguascalientes
Lagos de Moreno
GUANAJUATO
Dolores Hidalgo
León
Guanajuato
JALISCO
QUERÉTARO
San Miguel de Allende
Querétaro
La Piedad
Salamanca
Zamora
Morelia
Uruapan
Pátzcuaro
Zitácuaro
Toluca
MICHOACÁN
MÉXICO
Cacahuamilpa
Taxco
Iguala
Lázaro Cárdenas
GUERRERO
OCEANO PACIFICO
(PACIFIC OCEAN)